MEG'S MUMMY

by Helen Nicoll
and Jan Pieńkowski

PUFFIN BOOKS

Meg and Mog
went on an
expedition
to Egypt

They flew
up the Nile

and landed on a pyramid

Meg bandaged Mog up

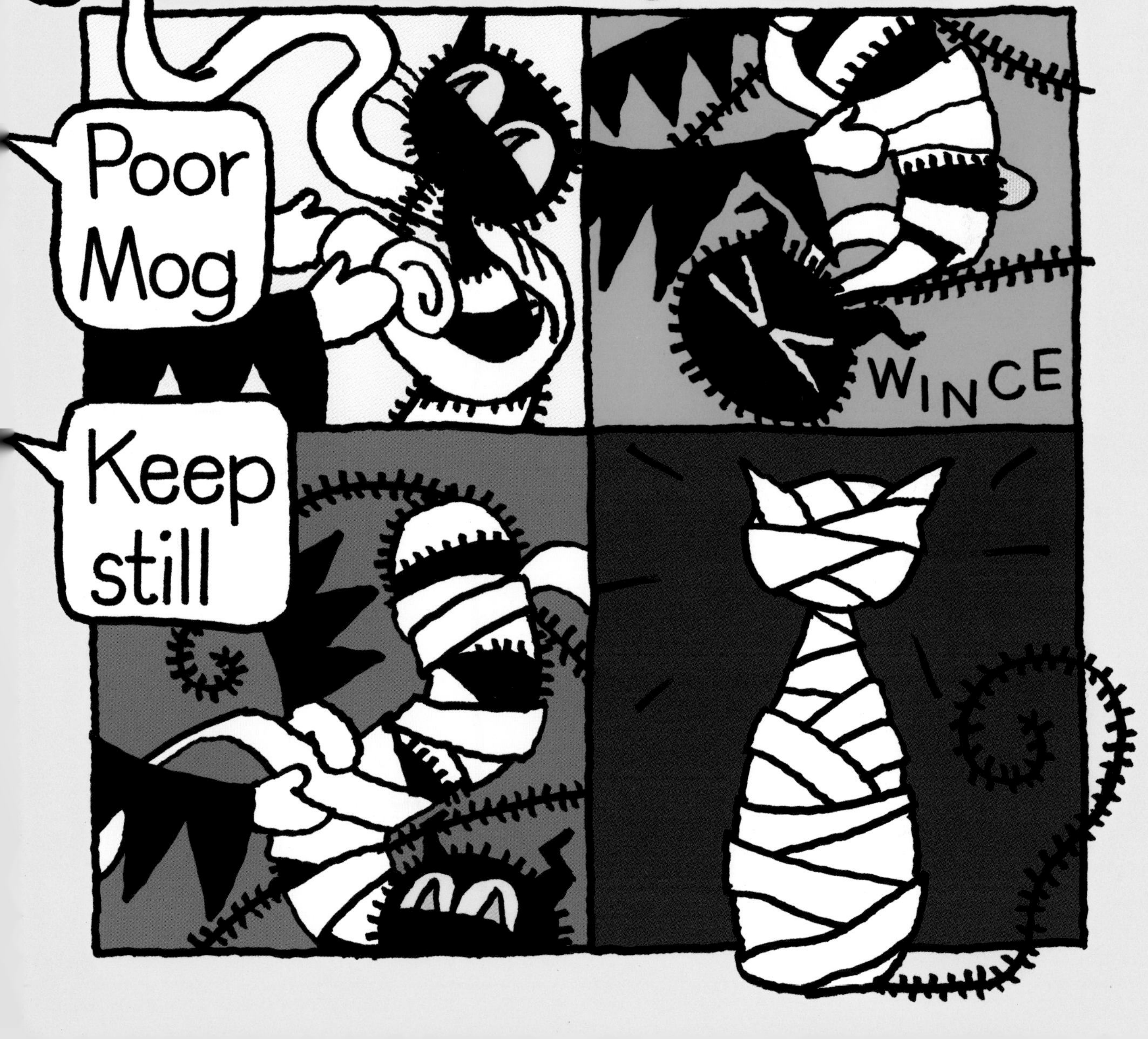

She peered
in the door

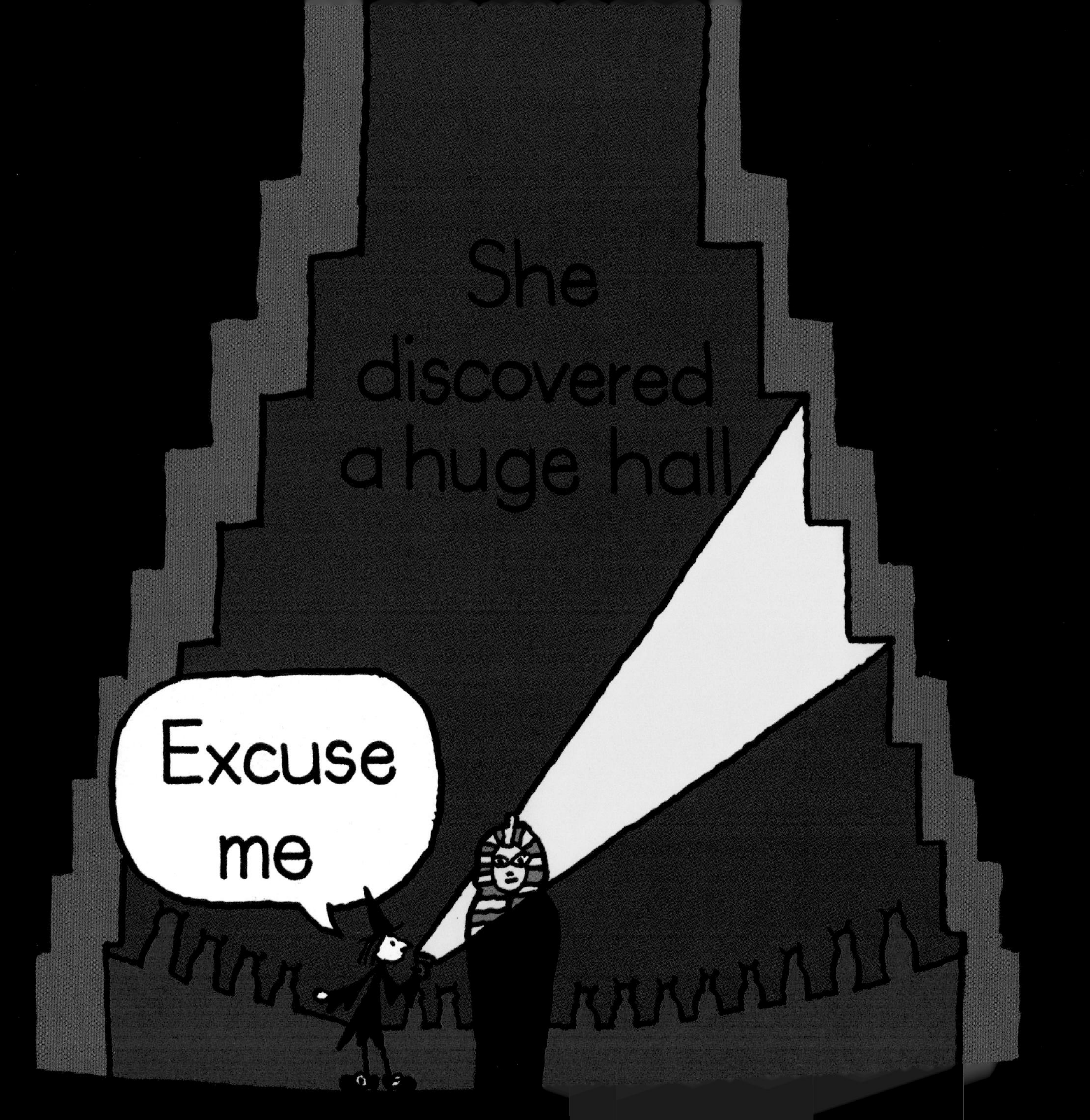
She discovered a huge hall
Excuse me

Mog's bandage had slipped

A boat appeared

It was a crocodile

Goodbye!

The Meg and Mog Books

for Kuba

PUFFIN BOOKS
Published by the Penguin Group: London, New York, Ireland, Australia, Canada, India, New Zealand and South Africa
Penguin Books Ltd, Registered Offices: 80 Strand, London WC2R 0RL, England
puffinbooks.com
First published 2004
Published in this edition 2006
10 9 8 7 6 5 4 3 2
Text copyright © Helen Nicoll, 2004
Illustrations copyright © Jan Pieńkowski, 2004
Story and characters copyright © Helen Nicoll and Jan Pieńkowski, 2004
All rights reserved
The moral right of the author and illustrator has been asserted
Lettering by Caroline Austin
Made and printed in Italy by Printer Trento Srl
British Library Cataloguing in Publication Data
A CIP catalogue record for this book is available from the British Library
ISBN 978-0-140-56978-0